Dear Parents:

Congratulations! Your child is taking the first steps on an exciting journey. The destination? Independent reading!

STEP INTO READING® will help your child get there. The program offers five steps to reading success. Each step includes fun stories and colorful art or photographs. In addition to original fiction and books with favorite characters, there are Step into Reading Non-Fiction Readers, Phonics Readers and Boxed Sets, Sticker Readers, and Comic Readers—a complete literacy program with something to interest every child.

Learning to Read, Step by Step!

Ready to Read   Preschool–Kindergarten
• big type and easy words • rhyme and rhythm • picture clues
For children who know the alphabet and are eager to begin reading.

Reading with Help   Preschool–Grade 1
• basic vocabulary • short sentences • simple stories
For children who recognize familiar words and sound out new words with help.

Reading on Your Own   Grades 1–3
• engaging characters • easy-to-follow plots • popular topics
For children who are ready to read on their own.

Reading Paragraphs   Grades 2–3
• challenging vocabulary • short paragraphs • exciting stories
For newly independent readers who read simple sentences with confidence.

Ready for Chapters   Grades 2–4
• chapters • longer paragraphs • full-color art
For children who want to take the plunge into chapter books but still like colorful pictures.

STEP INTO READING® is designed to give every child a successful reading experience. The grade levels are only guides; children will progress through the steps at their own speed, developing confidence in their reading. The F&P Text Level on the back cover serves as another tool to help you choose the right book for your child.

Remember, a lifetime love of reading starts with a single step!

For Danny, Kate, and Jane
—D.M.

Visit us on the Web!
StepIntoReading.com
rhcbooks.com

Educators and librarians, for a variety of teaching tools, visit us at RHTeachersLibrarians.com

Library of Congress Cataloging-in-Publication Data
Names: Murray, Diana, author. | Karipidou, Maria, illustrator.
Title: Pizza pig / by Diana Murray ; illustrated by Maria Karipidou.
Description: New York : Random House Children's Books, [2018] | Series: Step into reading.
Step 2 | Summary: Pig enjoys making just the right pizza to delight each of his customers,
so when Turtle will not eat he must figure out why.
Identifiers: LCCN 2017001666 (print) | LCCN 2017030186 (ebook) |
ISBN 978-1-5247-1334-8 (pb) | ISBN 978-1-5247-1335-5 (glb) | ISBN 978-1-5247-1336-2 (ebk)
Subjects: | CYAC: Stories in rhyme. | Pizza—Fiction. | Pigs—Fiction. | Animals—Fiction. |
Restaurants—Fiction.
Classification: LCC PZ8.3.M9362 (ebook) | LCC PZ8.3.M9362 Piz 2018 (print) | DDC [E]—dc23

Printed in the United States of America
10 9 8 7 6 5 4 3 2

This book has been officially leveled by using the F&P Text Level Gradient™ Leveling System.

Pizza Pig

by Diana Murray
illustrated by Maria Karipidou

Random House 🏠 New York

Pizza! Pizza!
What a dish.
Pig makes pizza
as you wish.

Shop is crowded
day and night.
Pig makes every pie
just right.

Hungry diners
take a seat.
Pizza! Pizza!
What a treat.

Bears get pizza
topped with jam.

Gulls get pizza
topped with clams.

Penguins like their pizza cold.

Rats want cheese
with extra mold.

Topped with carrots.

Topped with fish.

Pizza! Pizza!

As you wish!

Sloths lean back
and take it slow.

Monkeys eat it
on the go.

Poodles eat
while doing tricks.

Topped with tin cans.

Topped with twigs.

Topped with slop

for muddy pigs.

Eating.

Laughing.

Having fun!

Happy diners!

All but one. . . .

Pig makes every pie just right.

So why won't Turtle take a bite?

Pig is worried.

What is wrong?

Did he cook the worms

too long?

Did he undercook
the slugs?
Did he add
the fresh green bugs?

Turtle hides
inside her shell.
What is wrong?
It's hard to tell.

Perhaps a seaweed pie
instead?

Turtle peeks.

She shakes her head.

Pig brings out
another tray.
Turtle's shy.
She looks away.

Pig's tail droops.

What can he bring?

Pizza topped with
EVERYTHING?!

Turtle sinks down
in her seat.
What is wrong?
Why won't she eat?

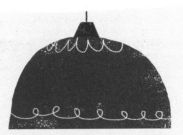

Pig looks here.

Pig looks there.

Then he spies

the empty chair!

Now he knows
just what to do!
Pizza! Pizza!
Made for two!

Hungry Pig
sits in the chair.
Pizza!
Best for friends
to share!

Turtle smiles
and takes a bite.
"Yum!" she says.
"This pie's just right!"